T is for Torture

Marie Lestrange

To all the freaks who dare to be their authentic, spooky selves— this book is for you.

*Disclaimer: This novel is fiction, except for the parts that aren't.

T is for Torture
Copyright © 2023 Marie Lestrange. All rights reserved. Crimson Cult Media supports the right to free expression and the value of copyright. The purpose of copyright is to encourage writers and artists to produce the creative works that enrich our culture. The scanning, uploading, reproduction, transmission in any form or by and means of distribution, electronic or mechanical, including photocopying, recording, or by any information storage or retrieval system of this book without written permission is a theft of the author's intellectual property. If you would like permission to use material from the book (other than for review purposes), please contact crimsoncultmedia@gmail.com. Thank you for your support of the author's rights. For more information please visit https://crimsoncultmedia.wixsite.com/crimson-cult-media

This book is for entertainment purposes only. It is not meant to be used as an instruction manual.

Printed in Oliver Springs, Tennessee, United States of America
Library of Congress Control Number: 2023935855

Description: Crimson Cult Media, 2023 | 32 pages of 4-color illustrations. | Series: Little Lestrange. | Audience: Adult. | Summary: Little Lestrange learns about the dark side of history by examining torture devices from A to Z.
Identifiers: LCCN 2023935855| ISBN: 979-8-9880338-0-6 (hardback) | ISBN: 979-8-9880338-1-3 (paperback) | ISBN: 979-8-9880338-37 (ebook)
Subjects: FICTION_HORROR, WIT AND HUMOR| Picture Books. |.BISAC: FIC015000, FIC016000, TRU010000

A is for Axe

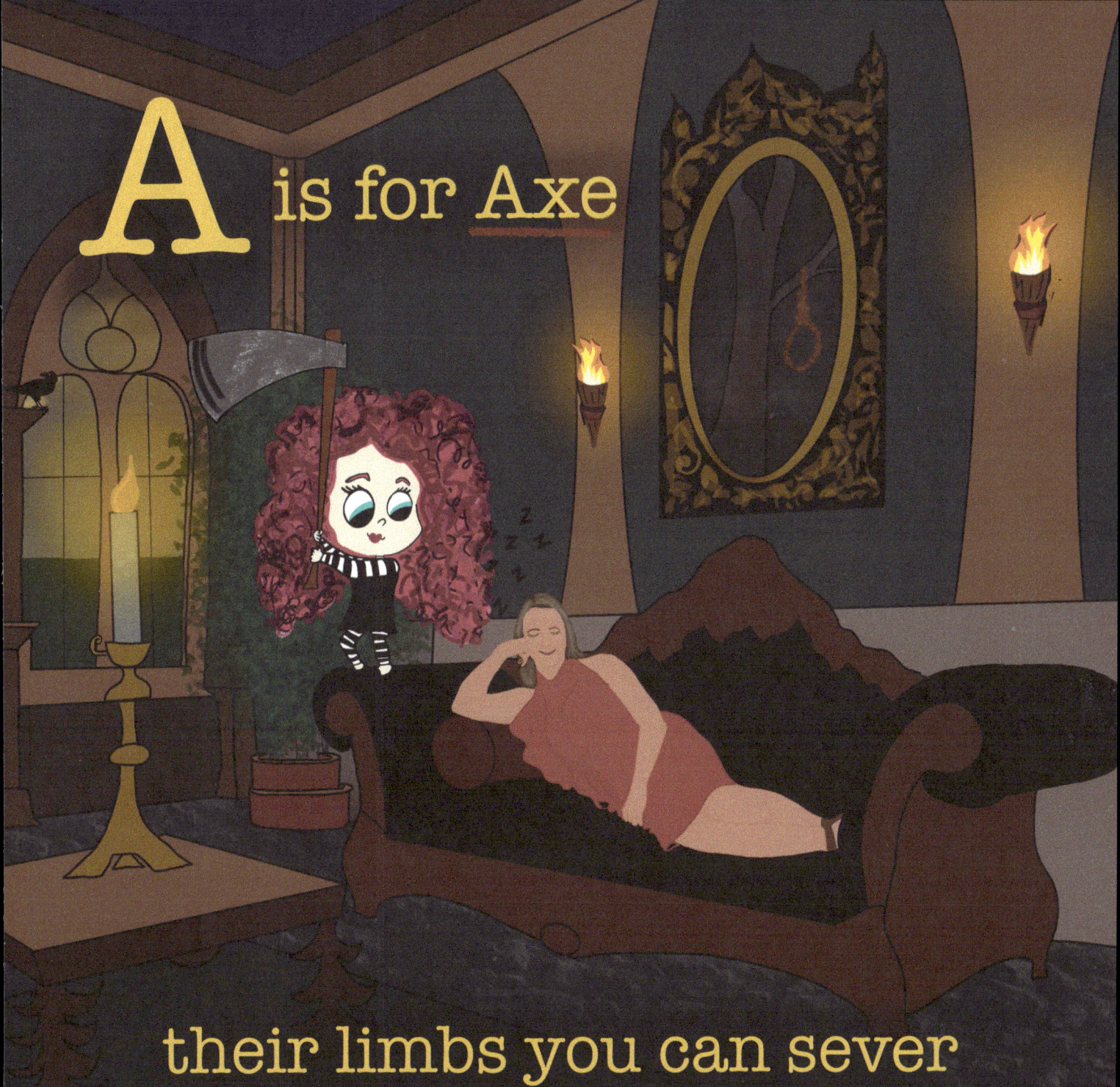

their limbs you can sever

B is for Breast ripper

a painful endeavor

C is for Cattleprod,

which comes with a shock

D

is for Ducking stool, much worse than the stock

Welcome Disorderly Women

E is for Exposure

often buried alive

F is for Flaying,
impossible to survive

G is for Gibbeting,

left alone to die

H is for Heretic's fork,

they'll confess to any lie

I is for Iron Maiden

spiked with nails on all sides

J is for Judas Cradle, a pointed edge they'll sit astride

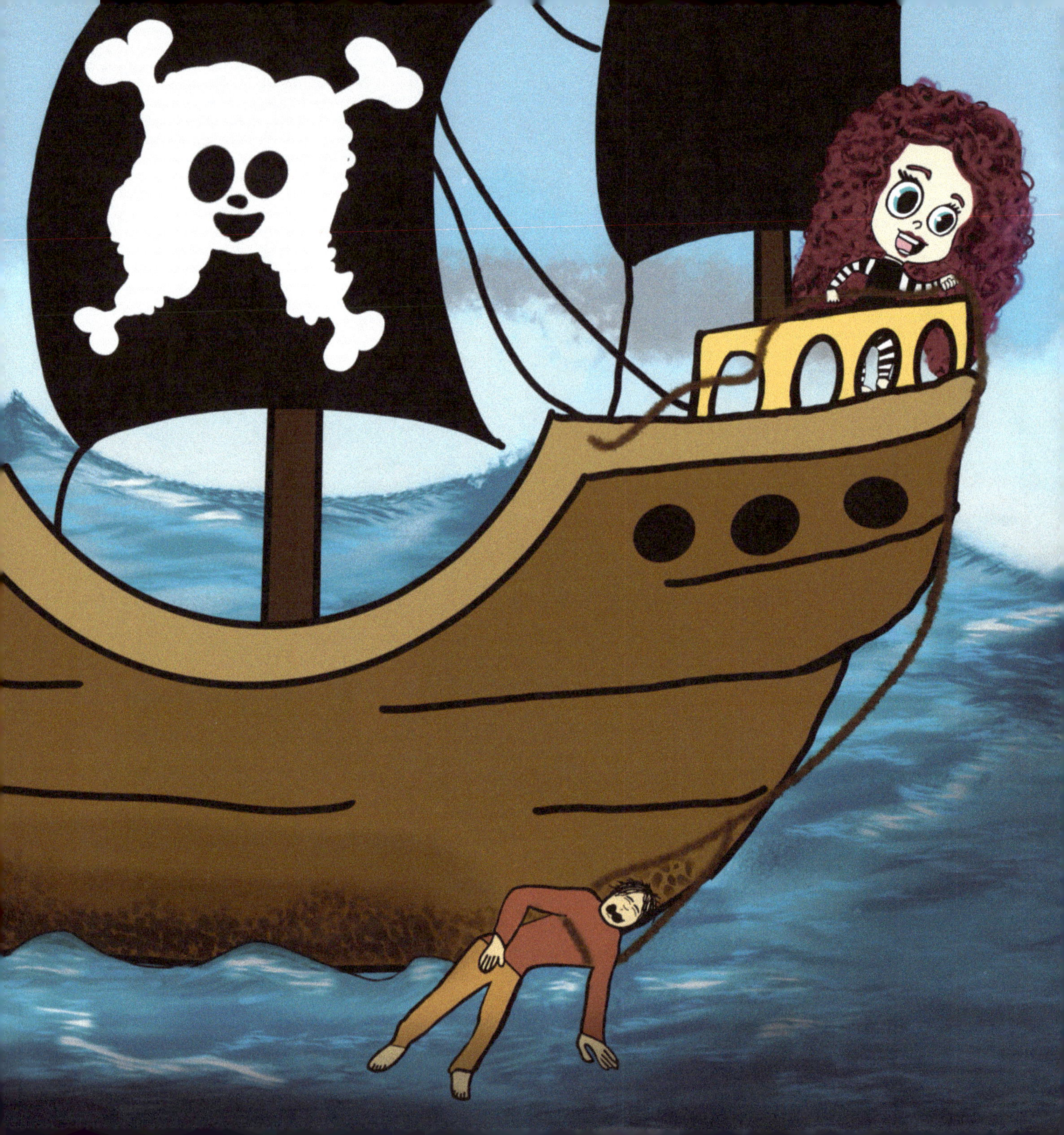

K is for Keelhauling, drag them under a ship

L is for Lead Sprinkler, molten metal you can drip

M is for Malay Boot,

to crush the foot or leg

N is for Nero's Roman candles

Burning while they beg

O is for Oil (boiled, that is!)

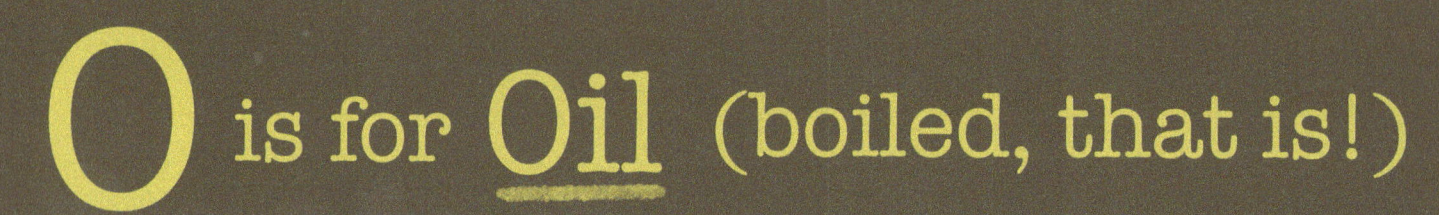

with a pulley, cauldron, and hook

P is for Pillory,
so all the town can look

Q is for Quartering,
torn limb from limb

R is for Rats,

their escape quite grim

S is for Scaphism,

a nasty affair

T is for The Rack

this one is fair

U is for Upended Sawing,
the blood leaves a trail

V is for Vlad

you, too, can impale!

W is for Breaking Wheel,

the pain is quite severe

X is for eXploitation,
clowns are her worst fear

Y is for Yawn,
no sleep is now his doom

Z is for the worst of all,
an endless meeting in ZOOM!

Pre-Order Now!

S is for Serial Killer

Marie Lestrange

FREE Downloadable Coloring Sheets:

https://dl.bookfunnel.com/98yd5u2noq